Harry McNairy, Tooth Fairy

Ann Fitzpatrick Alper

ILLUSTRATIONS BY Bridget Starr Taylor

Albert Whitman & Company

Morton Grove, Illinois

To Art, who gives and gives. —A. F. A.

To two of my best friends, Reed and Eli.
Love, Mom. —B. S. T.

Library of Congress Cataloging-in-Publication Data

Alper, Ann Fitzpatrick.
Harry McNairy, Tooth Fairy / by Ann Fitzpatrick Alper ;
illustrated by Bridget Starr Taylor.
p. cm.
Summary: Harry McNairy, the Tooth Fairy assigned to North
Mill Valley, is astounded when Michael refuses to trade in his
lost tooth for money.
ISBN 0-8075-3166-9
[1. Tooth Fairy—Fiction.] I. Taylor, Bridget Starr, 1959— ill.
II. Title.
PZ7.A4622Har 1998 [E]—DC21
98-13393 CIP AC

Harry the Tooth Fairy had more fun than most people. It was he who flew to the houses of children who lost a baby tooth. It was he who left money under their pillows while they slept. It was he who hid and saw smiles light up their faces when they found the money.

He didn't go to the houses of *all* the children in the world, of course. He just took care of North Mill Valley. Like other tooth fairies, Harry could fly right through screens and windows. He could slide his wonderfully flat fairy hands beneath pillows without ever waking a child.

On the night Ceci Rivera's first tooth fell out, Harry slid it from beneath her pillow and left a dollar in its place. What a wonderful present the tooth would be for his son, Barry! Though you may not know it, tooth fairies can't grow their own teeth. They have always depended on the baby teeth of strangers.

Harry flew directly home and
gave Barry the shiny tooth.
"Thank you, Papa, oh, thank you!" Barry
said. Then he pressed the tooth into his soft pink
bubble-gums next to the one he already had on the
bottom. "One more on top and I can have a cookie!"
Barry's little sister, Shary, watched with tears in her
eyes. Harry's wife, Mary, patted Shary's head. "She's so
tired of broccoli slushes and smashed-up tomatoes, Harry.
Shary needs another tooth so she can chew something!"

"You shall have the next one, Shary," Harry told her. "It will be Michael Madding's. His left front tooth on top is very loose and bound to fall out within days." Harry picked up his daughter and flew around the room. "You and Barry will soon be munching apples."

"And candy!" Barry added.

"And popcorn!" Shary shouted.

The evening Michael Madding's tooth fell out, Harry was outside the window before Michael even went to sleep. He hid behind the flowers, counting his money. "Sometimes these children fool a fairy," Harry murmured to himself. "Sometimes they lose *two* teeth. A good tooth fairy always has an extra dollar or two."

At last Michael was asleep.

Harry flew through the screen and stood beside Michael's bed. "What a lovely boy," he whispered to himself. "Almost as lovely as my Barry. I wonder why they didn't name him something nice, though, like Larry or Gary."

Harry slipped his hand under the pillow and felt all around. There was no tooth. "He's a hider," Harry muttered. Then he searched all through Michael's bed. No tooth.

He looked *in* the closet, *on* the toy shelves, and *under* the bed. No tooth! Harry had heard Michael's mother tell him to put the tooth under his pillow for the tooth fairy. Where was it?

Harry stayed around until the next morning and listened in on Michael and his friend Ceci in the backyard.

"How much did you get for your tooth?" Ceci asked.

"Nothing," Michael said. "I didn't put it under the pillow."

Ceci's eyes got round as cookies. "Why not?"

"Because," Michael answered.

Michael's mother stopped pulling weeds from her carrot patch. "That's not an answer, Michael. Why didn't you leave your tooth under the pillow?"

Michael shrugged. "I don't know. I guess I just want to keep it."

Harry flew directly back home and blurted, "Michael doesn't want to leave his tooth under the pillow. He wants to *keep* it!"

"WANTS TO *KEEP* IT!" Shary and Barry wailed. Pea pudding streamed from their mouths.

"Good heavens!" Mary cried. "This is terrible! There aren't many children in your territory, Harry dear. What shall we do for teeth if Michael Madding holds on to his?"

Harry took a deep breath. "I shall write him a note, Mary. That's what I'll do."

That evening, Harry showed his family what he'd written.
"This is a very good note, Harry," Mary said.
"Michael won't be able to resist a note like this," Barry added.
"Papa can really write notes," Shary said.

When Michael woke up the next morning, he found the note right away. He read as much of it as he could by himself. Then he took the note to his mother.

"What does this word say?" he asked.

"*Authorized*," his mother answered. "The tooth fairy is allowed to pay you a dollar for your tooth. He says you can't lose."

"I can lose my tooth," Michael muttered.

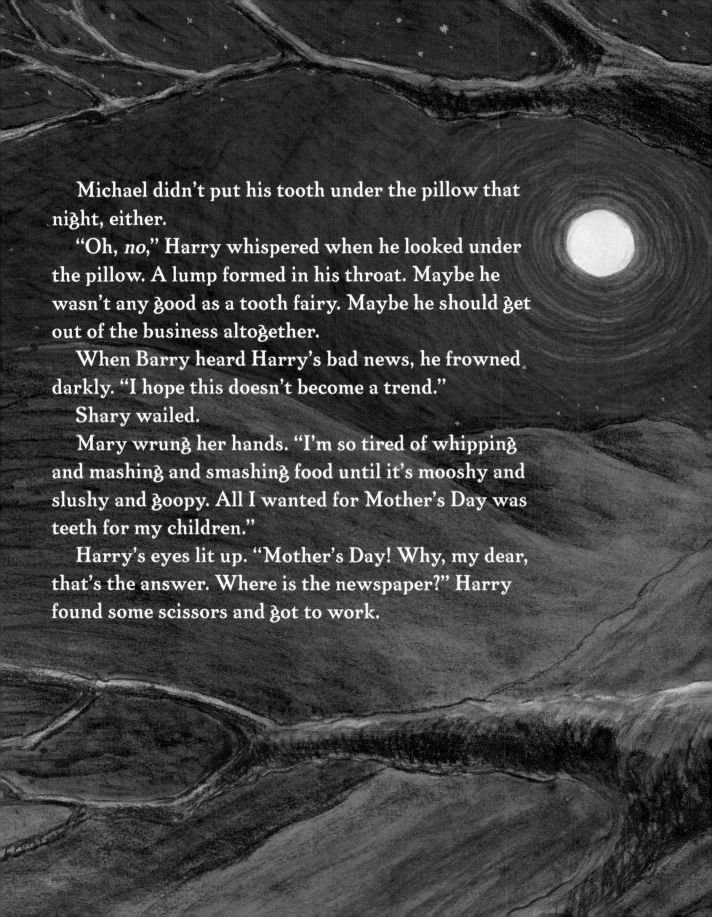

Michael didn't put his tooth under the pillow that
night, either.

"Oh, *no*," Harry whispered when he looked under
the pillow. A lump formed in his throat. Maybe he
wasn't any good as a tooth fairy. Maybe he should get
out of the business altogether.

When Barry heard Harry's bad news, he frowned
darkly. "I hope this doesn't become a trend."

Shary wailed.

Mary wrung her hands. "I'm so tired of whipping
and mashing and smashing food until it's mooshy and
slushy and goopy. All I wanted for Mother's Day was
teeth for my children."

Harry's eyes lit up. "Mother's Day! Why, my dear,
that's the answer. Where is the newspaper?" Harry
found some scissors and got to work.

When Michael woke up the next morning, he was puzzled by the pictures of jewelry, perfume, and boxes of candy cut from a newspaper. Then he saw the note. The words were so easy this time, he was able to read them slowly to himself.

Dear Michael,
Did you know
that Mother's Day
is only six days
away?
Harry T. McNair
Tooth Fairy

When Michael finished, he felt in his mouth and discovered another loose tooth. He went to the mirror and wiggled the tooth out.

That night he left two teeth under his pillow and a small note of his own.

Harry was delighted to leave three dollars.

Flying home, he did extra loops and twirls in the sky.
When he gave Shary and Barry their teeth, everyone hugged and danced around in a circle.
For dinner, the whole McNairy family had pizza.

On Mother's Day, when Michael gave his mother a beautiful box of candy, Harry was there. And when Michael's mother gave him a big hug, a tear of happiness rolled down Harry's cheek.

"Being a tooth fairy is the best job in the world," he said to himself.

He would be a tooth fairy forever.